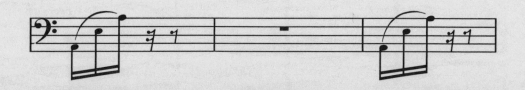

SPARKY
AND
THE MAGIC GARDEN

Julian R Eyers

SPARKY

AND
THE MAGIC GARDEN

BY

LUCIAN EYERS

Illustrated by the Author

Published by E'mage London 1994
Text and Illustrations © Lucian Eyers 1994

E'mage © 1994 Registered Trade Mark

A CIP catalogue record for this book is available
from the British Library

ISBN 1 898501 00 9

Printed in Great Britain by Cambus Litho Limited
Typeset by Brian Ransted

Dedicated to
Charmain and Ziad

This story is based on a character you may already know.

To those of you who have not been formally introduced to Sparky, you may easily find yourself mistaking her for a very ordinary black household cat.

In fact apart from her fine silky coat and little spark of white below her chin, she was like any black cat that may cross your path. For what made her special was that she feared nothing — least of all people, well, almost nothing as you will discover later. Now because of this she had something that a lot of cats and most people seem to miss in life and that was great adventures.

Do not be misled into thinking her whole life was full of excitement, for most of the week her owners kept Sparky locked in their house in the city.

They were not unkind to her for they loved her very much, spoiling her with such culinary delights as chicken liver pâté and smoked salmon.

It was only that the city was not the place for a special cat like Sparky. As there was no garden to play in, Sparky made the best of her life in her small uneventful home.

Often she would scale the curtains imagining she was climbing the bark of a tree. The indoor plants wished on many occasions Sparky had her own garden as she stalked her prey of passing feet, springing from the tired palms and geraniums.

In fact her passion for nibbling toes bore no bounds as she would creep under the bed covers and wrestle with the unwilling prey.

Even at bath time her paws would claw the water while she fished for a big toe. Now, some of you are thinking that this story is already becoming too far fetched and I can sense that you suspect I am making it up — well I am not. You are quite right in thinking that cats do not like water and if you are one of those disbelievers, let me just remind you Sparky was fearless!

Now early one Saturday morning Sparky awoke with excitement. She had spent the whole week counting the days on her soft paw. Leaping on the bed she attempted to stir her owners who had been enjoying a well deserved lie-in after a busy week. They could only manage a sleepy hello as they rolled further under the covers. However, Sparky was a determined cat. Sinking her teeth into a warm foot she reminded her friends that it was Saturday and that meant the beginning of her adventures.

Eventually after a few weary complaints and several cups of tea the two friends prepared Sparky's travel basket for the exciting journey into the countryside. The only thing that was missing was Sparky who was undoubtedly the most eager to go but who always enjoyed a game of hide and seek before they left.

There were not many rooms to hide in and so it was not long before her ears could be seen poking up from inside a large Greek urn.

When her friends had finished packing her basket with a soft cushion and a few nibbles for the journey, they slammed the front door behind them and strolled out into the bright sunshine.

No sooner had she tasted the city air and felt the gentle breeze upon her fur, than she was bundled into the back of a motor car where she spent the next few hours asleep in her basket. As you can imagine it is very difficult to have adventures in a small basket even for a clever cat like Sparky. So in these cramped situations it is far better to dream about them.

She was still asleep when they drove up the long gravel drive.

Not wishing to wake her they carried her gently past the two great hanging cedars and up a flight of stone steps to the door.

The brass knocker awoke her and as she adjusted her eyes she found herself being carried along a wide marble corridor. Then Sparky's door was opened and she stepped out to stretch her sleepy legs.

Two hands clasped themselves around her tummy and lifting her in the air her friends whispered to her in anticipation.

"We've got a big surprise for you little Sparky."

Through several rooms they carried her and along a dark passageway they went until they came to a noble doorway. It was dark although a stream of light shone through the lock and under the door. When it opened, Sparky's eyes filled with delight and she leapt from her friend's arms into the most magnificent garden she had ever seen.

She could hear the sound of running water in the distance. Quietly Sparky walked along a moss-covered stone path-way until she arrived at the source.

The young cat was startled and lay down on her tummy, for sticking out of a brick wall was the head of another cat much larger than her own. This cat was spewing cascades of water from its mouth — it took several minutes before Sparky realised the lion was only made of stone.

Our inquisitive little friend could not help herself from jumping up on the fountain and as she watched the splashing and bubbles in the pool, she noticed a small flash of orange darting amongst the weed. With one flick of her paw she scooped the water and out popped a tiny goldfish.

Now this is one side of cats I find unfortunate, however, we have to realise that they are natural hunters. I was also surprised, as you will probably be, when I tell you that before Sparky could as much as lick her lips, the little fish spoke to her.

"Oh great fearless feline please spare this bony bitter morsel that I am."

After a little thought she decided to speak. The fish was very privileged as Sparky would barely spare a word for her owners except the odd miaow.

"If I do, polite but tasty little fish, what will you do for me?"

"I will tell you where the plumpest, juiciest fish lives, but you must put me back first for I will certainly die without my pool to swim in."

Sparky had a good heart and a big appetite and so carefully she lifted the little fish back into the pool. After filling its gills with water the fish explained about a hole in a bush by a white gate which led to a large fish pond.

Quickly she bid the fish good day and shot down the garden path towards the white gate in the distance. At this point I should warn you that it is not a good idea to believe everything people or fish tell you, as Sparky was about to find out. The fish was quite right about the hole in the bush but there was certainly no sign of any fish pond. Just a small lawn with one chair and a garden table.

Suddenly a ferocious dog shot through the legs of the table, knocking over a jug of fruit juice which smashed to the ground. Sparky flew up a cherry tree and as the dog barked angrily she had to agree that her fearlessness did not stretch to large dogs with sharp teeth.

It was not long before a smile appeared on her tiny black face. The dog's raging owner scolded the dog and dragged him inside for breaking the jug and wasting his beverage.

I shall remember not to trust a goldfish again, she thought, as she jumped from the tree and ran back into the magic garden.

Sparky looked back at the house and the two grand cedars towering above.

She thought how thrilling it would be to charge across the massive stretch of lawn and so she did. Not wishing to stop she scampered up the trunk of the nearest cedar and viewed the garden from a high branch.

How lucky I am to be alive, she thought, and to be the queen of this magic kingdom.

For even cats have ideas of grandeur.

All of a sudden a flock of crows tried to attack her, but they were frightened off as she plucked a tail feather from one of them.

I will not let any trouble makers affect my adventures she decided and climbed down to explore the woodland below.

The woodland was thick with ivy and she could barely see where she was going. It was also dark and although cats are very good in the dark, she preferred the idea of lying on her back and soaking up the sun. She was just about to step onto the lawn again when a faint rustle could be heard on the edge of the woodland. Her curiosity always came before a cat nap so she decided to investigate.

Deep amongst a pile of old leaves sat the tiniest man Sparky had ever set her big green eyes on.

He had an enormous nose and an even bigger tummy. If it was not for his beard she could have mistaken him for a child. In fact, he could easily have been a dwarf but even Sparky knew there was no such thing, at least not in this story.

He pulled his boot off and shaking the soil from inside, noticed Sparky peering through the bushes.

"Hello Puss, come to give me a hand have you?"

Sparky looked in amazement as she had no intention of doing any work for this would most certainly interfere with her adventures.

She put her head to one side and the little man took this to mean, why are you here? He was quite right as that was precisely what she meant.

"Who else would look after this garden? The lawn doesn't cut itself you know. One hundred and sixty years I've been tending to these giant cedars, the grandest around they are. You won't see finer rhododendrons and that's because they're not just plants, they're friends. I will let you into a little secret young Puss. If you are thinking of a career looking after a magic garden, then I will tell you what you need — plenty of hard work and good conversation."

Sparky gave a short miaow, she had already been told untruths by a cheeky goldfish and was not going to be taken in by a little old man claiming he was over one hundred and sixty years old.

"So you don't believe me!" cried the old man who admittedly had a very good understanding of cat tongue.

"I can see you need a little reassurance. When the sun falls behind that silver birch, come back and bring a musical instrument you can play to me."

She went off feeling very strange, apart from hearing her own language from a human she had not a single idea what instrument she would play for him.

Eventually Sparky found an old washboard and dragged it to the spot where the little man had met her.

When she arrived all the leaves had been swept away and the sunlit clearing was packed with every woodland animal imaginable.

The noise was quite unbearable as the little man sat amongst a family of arguing hedgehogs and badgers, while trying to instruct the birds in the branches to keep in time.

Suddenly everyone became quiet as they all turned to look at the newcomer. Sparky turned around also and not seeing anyone behind her realised they were all looking at her.

" **A**h you've arrived at last",
exclaimed the little old man,
waving his willow baton at Sparky.

"You can perch next to the
string section, Otter will prompt
you when your washboard skills are
required."

No sooner had she squeezed
herself between a prickly hedgehog
and a rather fat otter, the baton
was raised. A slim stoat summoned
up a charming solo on a flute made
from a bright yellow reed. Then the
blackbirds joined in, all harmonising
together in a sweet serenade. After
a few minutes the hedgehogs slowly
pulled back the bows to their violins
and the most delightful tune
emerged.

Sparky had never seen a woodmouse playing a clarinet. If she had not seen it with her own sharp eyes, she would have surely been as sceptical as you probably are at this moment.

Otter seemed to be putting everything into his performance as his whole body quivered with every stroke of his double bass. He got so excited at one point that he knocked Sparky in the ribs with his bow. She quickly struck the washboard with her paws, not knowing if this was her cue to start playing.

To Sparky's surprise the music was divine even to her high standards, for she was used to hearing only the finest Schubert sonatas. The little man now had his eyes closed as he swayed to the haunting melody of the badgers' French horns.

It was an enchanting picture to behold. All the animals seemed sublimely happy together, bringing beautifully inspiring music to everyone. Sparky put her chin in the air and gazing around thought to herself, this truly is a magical garden.

Sparky spent many happy days visiting the Magic Garden. To this very day if you listen carefully on a still afternoon, when the breeze upon the leaves subsides, the music of the animals and birds can be heard — and the tapping of Sparky's paws upon her rickety old washboard.